About Amphibians

Also in the ABOUT... series

About Birds
About Mammals
About Reptiles
About Insects
About Fish
About Arachnids
About Crustaceans

About Amphibians
A Guide for Children

Cathryn Sill

Illustrated by John Sill

PEACHTREE
ATLANTA

For the One who created amphibians.

—Genesis 1:1

Published by
PEACHTREE PUBLISHERS
1700 Chattahoochee Avenue
Atlanta, Georgia 30318-2112
www.peachtree-online.com

Text © 2001 Cathryn P. Sill
Jacket and interior illustrations © 2001 John C. Sill

First trade paperback edition published 2004

Jacket illustration by John Sill
Watercolor on archival quality 100% rag watercolor paper

Manufactured in Singapore

10 9 8 7 6 5 4 3 2 (hardcover edition)
10 9 8 7 6 5 4 3 2 1 (trade paperback edition)

Cataloging-in-Publication Data

Sill, Cathryn P., 1953–
    About amphibians: a guide for children / Cathryn Sill; illustrated by John Sill.
        p. cm.

    ISBN 1-56145-234-3 (hardcover)
    ISBN 1-56145-312-9 (trade paperback)

    I. Amphibians—Juvenile literature. [I. Amphibians.] I. John Sill, ill. Title.

QL644.2S48 2001
597.8—dc21   00-051034

About Amphibians

Amphibians have soft, moist skin.

PLATE 1
Red Salamander

Most amphibians spend part of their lives in water…

PLATE 2
Bullfrog

and part on land.

PLATE 3
Couch's Spadefoot Toad

Amphibians hatch from eggs laid in water or wet places.

They change as they grow into adults.

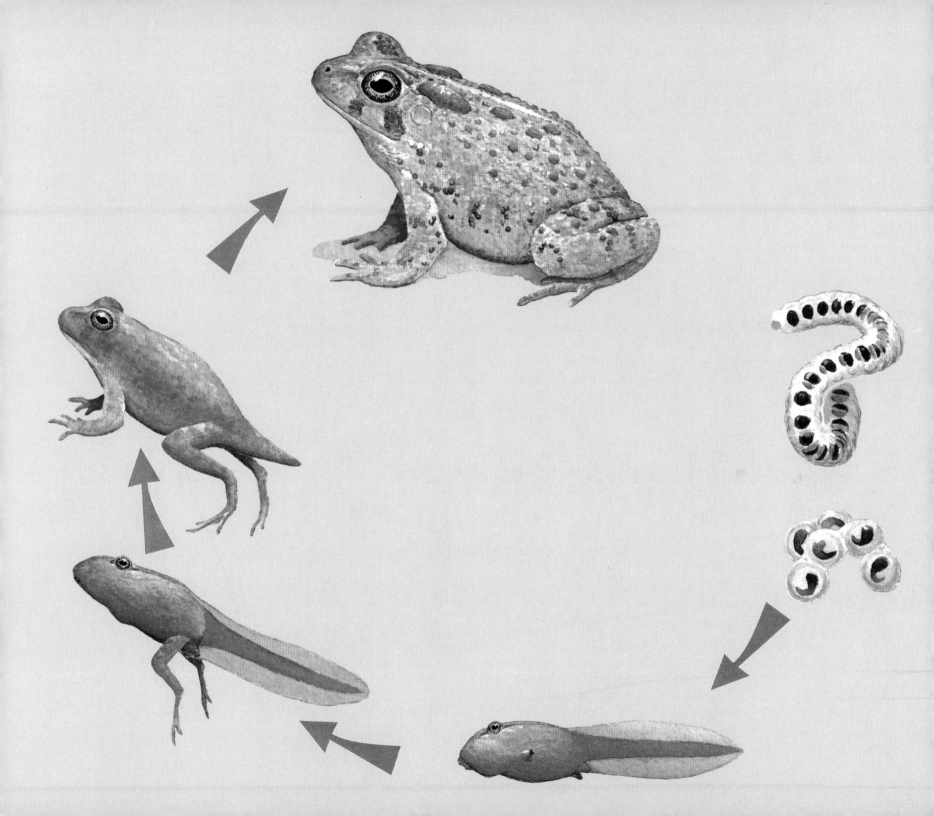

Some amphibians have tails.

Others lose their tails as they grow up.

PLATE 7
Eastern Narrowmouth Toad

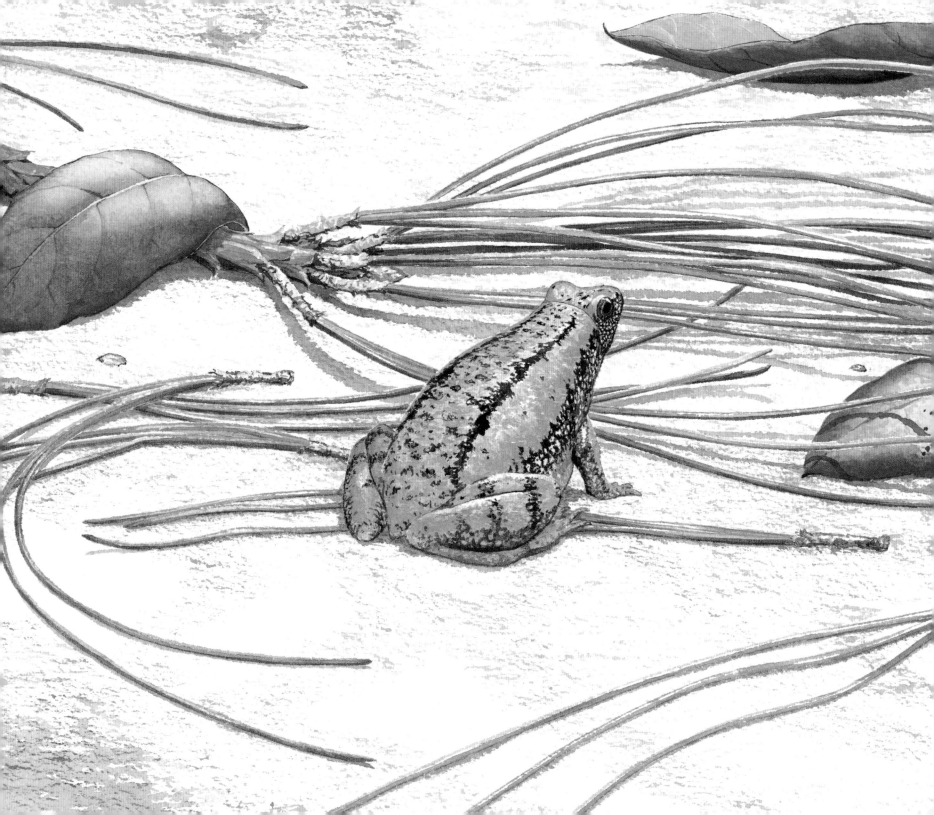

Amphibians have many enemies.

PLATE 8
Northern Leopard Frog

Some are camouflaged for protection.

PLATE 9
Gray Tree Frog

Others are protected by poison glands in their skin.

PLATE 10
Colorado River Toad

Amphibians bury themselves and sleep through very cold or very hot weather.

Some amphibians have voices and call to each other.

PLATE 12
Spring Peeper

Most amphibians eat insects.

Some may eat snakes, worms, and other small animals.

PLATE 14
Tiger Salamander

It is important to protect amphibians and the places where they live.

Afterword

PLATE 1
Amphibians have glands that secrete mucus to protect their skin and keep it moist. They can also breathe through their skin, and water passes in and out through it. Red Salamanders (3 to 7 inches long) live in clear, cool streams or under nearby leaves, rocks, or logs.

PLATE 2
The word "amphibian" comes from a Greek word that means "living two lives." Most amphibians live in water when they are young and on land as adults. The Bullfrog (3 1/2 inches long) is North America's largest frog. Bullfrogs are usually found in the plants growing at the edge of ponds, lakes, or streams.

PLATE 3
While some amphibians remain in water as adults, most live on land. Almost all return to water to have young. Spadefoot toads get their name from a sharp-edged "spade" on their back feet that allows them to dig down into sandy or loose soil. Couch's Spadefoots (2 1/4 to 3 1/2 inches long) are able to tolerate dry conditions and even semidesert by staying underground.

PLATE 4
Amphibian eggs are covered with a clear, slippery jelly that protects them. The eggs hatch into tadpoles or larvae. Spotted Salamanders (6 to 9 3/4 inches long) lay about one hundred eggs in a mass. They attach the egg mass to branches and stems in the water.

PLATE 5

The process of change amphibians go through is called metamorphosis. During this change, most grow legs and lungs so they can live on land. American Toads (2 1/4 inches long) have a long musical trill that is commonly heard in spring in much of eastern North America.

PLATE 6

Salamanders have a slender body, a long tail, and usually four legs that are about the same length. The tail of a Longtail Salamander (4 to 7 1/2 inches long) is nearly two-thirds of its total length.

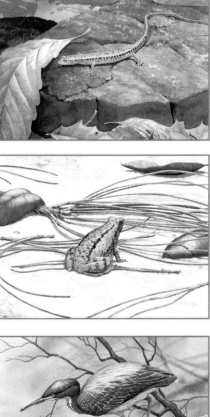

PLATE 7

When a tadpole develops into a frog or a toad, it loses its tail and develops long hind legs that enable it to jump or hop. Eastern Narrowmouth Toads are small (1 to 1 1/2 inches long), nocturnal toads that eat mostly ants.

PLATE 8

Many animals, including birds, snakes, and mammals, eat adult amphibians. Fish and other small water animals eat amphibian larvae. When fleeing an enemy, the Northern Leopard Frog (2 to 4 3/8 inches long) makes zigzag leaps until it reaches the safety of water.

PLATE 9

Many amphibians are able to hide from their enemies because of their protective coloration. Some have bright colors that warn enemies that they taste bad. The skin of the Gray Tree Frog (1 1/4 to 2 1/2 inches long) can change from gray to green in order to match its environment.

PLATE 10

The warts on a toad's skin have glands that give off a poison that burns the mouth and throat of any animal that tries to eat it. Toads do not cause people to have warts. The Colorado River Toad (3 to 6 inches long) is a very poisonous toad. A dog would probably be paralyzed or even die after biting this toad.

PLATE 11

Because amphibians are cold-blooded, their body temperature is the same as their surroundings. They become inactive by hibernating in very cold weather and estivating when the weather is hot and dry. Wood Frogs (1 3/8 to 3 1/4 inches long) are the only North American frogs to live above the Arctic Circle. Great Plains Toads (2 to 4 1/2 inches long) are able to live in drier habitats by burrowing down into loose soil.

PLATE 12

The calls of male frogs and toads attract mates and warn other males to stay away. This sound is made by a vocal pouch located in the throat. The song of the Spring Peeper (3/4 to 1 3/8 inches long) can be heard up to a half mile away and is one of the first signs of spring in North America.

PLATE 13

Frogs and toads capture insects by flicking their tongues out. Once the prey is stuck to the tongue, it is quickly pulled into the mouth. Oak Toads (3/4 to 1 1/4 inches long) are the smallest toads in North America.

PLATE 14

Amphibians swallow their food whole. The small teeth of some amphibians are used only to grasp and hold their prey. Tiger Salamanders (6 to 13 3/8 inches long) are the world's largest terrestrial salamanders.

PLATE 15

Amphibians are very beneficial. Many eat insects that destroy crops and carry disease. They provide food for other animals and are used in scientific research and education. Some experts believe that the declining numbers of amphibians indicate problems in our environment. We can protect amphibians like the Pine Barrens Tree Frog (1 1/8 to 2 inches long) by preserving the wetlands where they live.

Cathryn Sill is an elementary school teacher in Franklin, North Carolina, and the author of the acclaimed ABOUT… series. With her husband John and her brother-in-law Ben Sill, she coauthored the popular bird-guide parodies, A FIELD GUIDE TO LITTLE-KNOWN AND SELDOM-SEEN BIRDS OF NORTH AMERICA, ANOTHER FIELD GUIDE TO LITTLE-KNOWN AND SELDOM-SEEN BIRDS OF AMERICA, and BEYOND BIRDWATCHING, all from Peachtree Publishers.

John Sill is a prize-winning and widely published wildlife artist who illustrated the ABOUT… series and coauthored the FIELD GUIDES and BEYOND BIRDWATCHING. A native of North Carolina, he holds a B.S. in Wildlife Biology from North Carolina State University.